KU-743-051

Flora
McQuack

First published in 2002 by
Franklin Watts
96 Leonard Street
London
EC2A 4XD

Franklin Watts Australia
56 O'Riordan Street
Alexandria
NSW 2015

Text © Penny Dolan 2002
Illustration © Kay Widdowson 2002

A CIP catalogue record for this book is available
from the British Library.

ISBN 0 7496 4475 3 (hbk)
ISBN 0 7496 4621 7 (pbk)

Series Editor: Louise John
Series Advisor: Dr Barrie Wade
Cover Design: Jason Anscomb
Design: Peter Scoulding

Printed in Hong Kong

Flora McQuack bustled along the water's edge. There, in the tall grass beside the loch, sat the McPeck sisters.

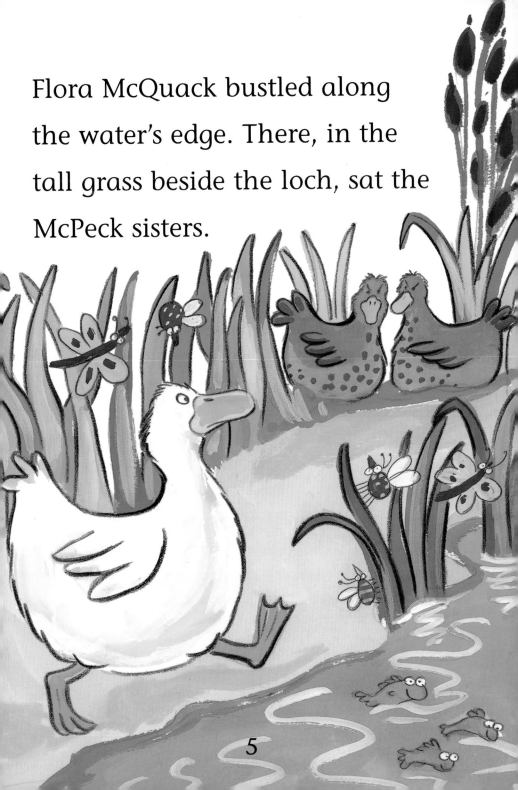

"Hello, lassies!" Flora cried.

"Sssssss…" they hissed. "Get away from our nests. Everyone knows you're a bad luck duck!"

"Meanies! I wouldn't hurt a tadpole," Flora hissed back.

7

Flora moved away but she had tears in her eyes. She thought of the McPeck sisters and the smooth eggs in their nests.

Flora sighed. Never, in all her life, had she laid an egg.

Flora waddled off around the loch, all alone.

Suddenly, she noticed something smooth and oval among the stones on the bank.

"Goodness me!" she exclaimed.

"It's a poor orphaned egg."

Flora nestled warmly against it.

"Ha, ha! You silly duck," laughed the McPeck sisters as they swam past. "That will never hatch."

"Och, mind your own business,"
quacked Flora. "It's my egg now
and I'm going to hatch it, no
matter how long it takes."

It took a very long time. Spring turned to summer and all the other eggs had hatched.

No sound came from Flora's egg
but still she sat on it patiently.

17

At last Flora heard something.
First a tapping, then a creaking
and a cracking and, finally, the
shell broke open.

The strange creature opened surprised eyes. It had four stumpy legs, a long tail and no feathers. It did not look like a duck at all!

"Mama!" cried the little creature, stumbling towards Flora.

"Och," exclaimed Flora, "you are a strange wee thing, but I love you!"

Flora marched to the edge of the loch. "Come along now," she said to her new baby. "Time for a swimming lesson."

Splash! Flora plunged into the
water and the little creature
followed her.

When Flora looked behind her, her new baby had disappeared beneath the ripples.

"Och, no! I've drowned the wee thing!" she gasped.

But up popped the little creature, water-weed dripping from its mouth. Gurgling happily, it dived again. Flora gazed at the trail of sparkling bubbles.

The McPeck sisters would never
be able to make fun of such a
good swimmer.

Up it popped again, splashing
Flora joyfully.

"Mind your manners," she scolded gently. "Don't behave like a little monster!"

And away swam Flora and her strange, long-necked baby across the wide waters of Loch Ness.

Hopscotch has been specially designed to fit the requirements of the National Literacy Strategy. It offers real books by top authors and illustrators for children developing their reading skills.

There are five other Hopscotch stories to choose from:

Marvin, the Blue Pig
Written by Karen Wallace, illustrated by Lisa Williams
Marvin is the only blue pig on the farm. He tries hard to make himself pink but nothing seems to work. Then, one day, his friend Esther gives him some advice...

Plip and Plop
Written by Penny Dolan, illustrated by Lisa Smith
Plip and Plop are two pesky pigeons that live in Sam's grandpa's garden. If anyone went out, Plip and Plop got busy... So Sam has to think of a way to get rid of them!

The Queen's Dragon
Written by Anne Cassidy, illustrated by Gwyneth Williamson
The Queen is fed up with her dragon, Harry. His wings are floppy and his fire has gone out! She decides to find a new one, but it's not quite as easy as she thinks...

Naughty Nancy
Written by Anne Cassidy, illustrated by Desideria Guicciardini
Norman's little sister Nancy is the naughtiest girl he knows. When Mum goes out for the day, Norman tries hard to keep Nancy out of trouble, but things don't quite go according to plan!

Willie the Whale
Written by Joy Oades, illustrated by Barbara Vagnozzi
Willie the Whale decides to go on a round-the-world adventure – from the South Pole to the desert and even to New York. But is the city really the place for a big, friendly whale?